Angel & Devil

Third person's POV

Our story begins sixty years after the celestial war between Angels and Devils there everlasting hatred for each other had finally taken them to the human realm. Paula's small human girl ended the brutal war by singing a peaceful song that touched the Angel queens hardened heart with a simple act of kindness. Soon the Devil king's twisted heart became pure. They finally saw the damage that their hatred had caused the two monarchs then sought to make amends and decided to live alongside the humans. Hence, on that day, the pact between Angels Devils and Humans forever sealed; now, the three races live together on earth peacefully, helping one another to be intense, searching for a future where everyone is happy.

Anyway, our story begins in New York City, the third-largest Angel City in the USA. Still, we're going to an individual home, preferably the manner of Lord and Lady Rose, who governs the city alongside Duke Sombra, but inside the walls of the Mansion where a young boy sits in his room alone and board eagerly waiting for something to happen and now we begin.

Michael's POV

I laid on my bed reading one of my favorite books for the third time today since I can't go outside; Mother and Father forbid me from leaving the manner, so I mainly read all day and, on occasion, stare out the window to look at the other boys at play. Still, then I hear someone knocking at the door. I then sit up on my bed and say, "come in" when the door opens, I see my sister Mimiru; she smiles at me and says, "hi, little bro, just wanted to be the first to wish you happy birthday here a small piece of cake."

My sister and my nanny primarily raised me, and today was supposed to be a happy day. Still, for me, it was another day in prison and another day when my parents would say they were proud of me, and they're so glad for me when they couldn't care less whether I lived or died. However, I heard the word surprise, and yet again, that would be another lie sigh.

Soon Mimiru and I walk downstairs and see mother and Father in the sitting room doing some office work. Mimiru nudged my shoulder and pointed to our little getaway that led outside the manner Mimiru gave me a small amount of money and said, have fun. I smiled at my sister and hugged her before leaving the Mansion.

Once I'm outside, I started walking down the street to a little pub I heard some servants called the Misty Chalis. Since I was now eighteen years old, I could enter without any problems. As I entered,

I saw a lot of people dancing and downright having fun. Still, I also saw an awful lot of spoiled snobs, so I mainly sat by the bar for most of the evening until someone sat next to me. He had amethyst colored hair and great violet eyes, and his haircut was short and smooth; he smiled at me and said, "hi angel face you new in town" I blushed and shook my head no "so do you live around here" I then said "yes my name is Michael Rose" the man smiled and said, "what a cute name mines Luke Moto.

I smiled at him and said, "well, nice to meet you, Luke what do you say we go somewhere else" Luke then nodded and grabbed my hand and lead me out of the pub and towards the central park, a place I wanted to visit Luke showed me all the pretty flowers and trees soon I smiled at him. I said, "umm can we be friends, Luke" Luke just smiled at me and said, "sure care to meet at the pub tomorrow" I smiled wide and nodded my head and ran home happy that I made a brand new friend as I returned home I saw that the party had almost started so I quickly ran upstairs. I found my best tuxedo put it on.

I then Came back downstairs and mingled with the guests; it was all pretty dull, though, so I mainly sat upstairs the entire time; then, my sister came into my room. She gave me my only present of the night as it was a small charm necklace that read peacefully. I smiled and hugged my sister and mainly spent time with her for the entire night. Then the next day came, I immediately got dressed in some casual clothes and waited till it was midday to return to the pub. Once the time date set, I escaped the manner and returned to the Misty Chalis waiting for Luke. Sure enough, he came, and I smiled so wide.
Luke's POV

Today I planned to take Michael out to my favorite shop. It was an art shop called the White Clay House that held many beautiful treasures, but we left the art shop. I gave Michael a little present. It was a touch phone so that he and I could talk and arrange more outings like this. As soon as Michael got the phone, he jumped up and down and hugged me. Of course, I chuckled as we continued our walk down the street to one of my favorite restaurants. It was called the Frozen Tulip Dinner. We sat at the table just talking to each other about anything that came up like music and hobbies, and soon I realized we had a lot in common with each other, which made me like him even more.

I then told Michael that I was a devil which made him blush when I asked him why he was blushing he said "because I'm an angel and angel's and devil's don't be-" i then interrupted Michael by placing my hand on his knee and whispering "so what all that matters is that weir happy together" Michael then moved in and kissed my lips catching me off guard and soon I embraced him and when we left the diner something new had formed between us a new but slightly frail bond but the joyous occasion was cut short by a man in white approaching us and saying "young master please come with me your mother and father are worried sick so please come with me" Michael then cringed at the mere mention of the words mother and Father that's when i stepped in and said "hey he's not going anywhere with you now get out of here" the man just glared at me and said "that wasn't a question" soon the man grabbed Michael's arm and dragged him into his car I tried to stop him but he put a gun to my head and said "don't even try it" I then backed off and saw how sad Michael looked in the window obviously something was up and I wasn't going to let him go through it alone so I flagged down a cab and told the driver to follow the car up ahead and soon I found myself before the Rose Mansion.

I snuck my way past the guards, looked through the bay window, and saw Michael being beaten ruthlessly by his Father. Honest to God, it broke my heart, and when the beating was over, he was carried upstairs to his room. I took the opportunity to text him. He responded immediately, saying.

"Hi Luke;-;"

"You okay, angel face):>."

"I'm fine, just a little sore. What are you doing right now?"

"Trying to find a way to get to you."

"!"

"No, Luke, don't my Father will kill you. Just get out of here."

"I can't just sit at home while my friend gets beaten just for being who he is, so I'm coming up there. That's the end of it."

"K"

Soon Michael leads me to his bedroom window, and Michael was able to fashion a rope out of his bedsheets that was enough to let me inside. I inspected the room around me and saw that it was reasonably cute, just like Michael, sitting on the bed in tears. I took note of this and sat next to him and placed my arm on Michael's shoulder, soothing him "angel face, why would your parents do that to you" I whispered into Michael's ear, wiping a stray tear away "because they don't care about me. They just adopted me for the public image they couldn't care less whether I lived or died," Michael cried.

I then hugged Michael, and Michael hugged me back, "then why don't you come live with me," I suggested. Michael's eyes began to sparkle as he looked up and said, "really," I nodded my head, and he quickly went to work getting his stuff together. Once everything was packed, Michael left a note for his sister, and we escaped out the window and made our way to my apartment.

Third person's POV

As the seasons rolled by both Michael and Luke grew closer and closer until they became lovers and Luke started noticing that Michael was slowly getting happier and happier the more time they spent together soon Michael forgot all about his terrible life with his family but one day Michael's sister Mimiru had tracked him down and greeted him with open arms she was proud that he had escaped that terrible setting so to celebrate she gave him a very special gift two train tickets to Atlanta Georgia once she delivered the gift she left but one fateful tuesday night Michael and Luke planned a fantastic date night but Luke was late to the restaurant and when he did arrive he was a sweaty mess but he still looked sharp as ever after dinner Michael got up to use the bathroom giving Luke the perfect opportunity to slip a little surprise into Michael's drink when Michael took a sip of his drink he felt something hard shift onto his tongue it wasn't an ice cube it had a metallic taste to it and when Michael spat it out it was a gorgeous silver ring that made Michael's eyes sparkle with such glamour he then looked at Luke who smiled mischievously and said "so yes or no" Michael began to cry tears of joy yelling "yes yes a thousand times yes Luke yes"

Luke and Michael then left the restaurant and returned home. They undid the lock and went into their shared bedroom. Luke then unleashed his horns and tail while Michael released his angel wings. They both stared at each other with lust in their eyes, and soon the two knew that the V card was about to be swiped, so they dimmed down the lights and undid the sheets tee hee.

Third person's POV

Michael and Luke got married without incident, and soon they moved to Atlanta to get away from all the city noise. They bought a cute house in the suburbs, and the two quickly started planning their future together, but they did take a break at times to spend time with one another like the time they went to Rita's one sweltering summer day the two then spent time talking to one another, and people watch

Michael's POV

I awoke to the smell of bacon and eggs coming from the kitchen. Slowly I began to stir and wake up entirely soon. I was downstairs sitting in the dining room where Luke had already set the plates. Then he put the bacon and eggs on our plates. When Luke finished with the Dishes, Luke kissed my lips. I smiled cutely, then he put the pan in the sink and returned to the dining room where we had breakfast "so how did you sleep, angel face" Luke asked, smiling at me. I smiled back and said, "just fine, but I did have a strange dream though" Luke raised a brow and said, "really about what" I shrugged and said, "something about cats or something."

Luke chuckled and said, "well, as long as you didn't have a nightmare" when we finished breakfast me and Luke decided to go for a walk around the neighborhood, I got dressed in some skinny blue jeans and a golden t-shirt. In contrast, Luke got dressed in a skull and bones shirt, a light jacket, and black cardigans. Once we got dressed, we went out. It was still early, so no one was out, yet we soon came to a little park small enough for small children to play on. It was so cute. As we walked home, there was a slight chill in the air that caused me to shiver, Luke then placed his jacket on me, and I blushed at the kind gesture. I then looked up at Luke and gave him a big kiss, and when we got home, Luke picked me up bridal style and carried me upstairs to our bedroom, where we cuddled for a while.

Soon Luke left for work, leaving me alone for a little bit, so I decided to do some housework funny because I never had to lift a finger back at the manor, but now that I'm with Luke, I know I can do anything tee hee.

As I took out the trash i saw a poster that read puppies for sale it was a small sale not to far from here so i thought i might surprise Luke with a new pet around the house so i quickly got in my car picked up a bag of dog food and dog toys and a doggie bed and a collar after I got everything I drove to the house where they were giving away the puppies and saw there was only one puppy left I smiled and got out of the car and walked up to the man selling them he was a sweet old man who smiled at me and said "hello lad you came just in time would you care to inspect this fine girl" I then picked up the small puppy who wiggled her tail as I held her in the air I then brought her close to my chest and she nuzzled against me and started licking my face I Giggled and she yipped i then turned to the old man and said "i'll take her how much do i owe you" the man smiled and said "no she's free of charge think of it as a gift" i then thanked the old man and carried the small puppy to the car where i gave her the collar i picked out and wrote the name Tulip on it and said "that'll be your name, sweety then i drove home dog in toe and Tulip then ran to the house while I carried all her stuff inside as I set everything up Tulip was resting in the living room I finished everything in time for Luke to arrive as soon as Luke opened the door he was instantly greeted by Tulip he smiled as the small German Shepherd jumped up at his fingers Luke then picked up Tulip and said "now where did you come from" I then snickered as I yelled "guilty" and Luke rolled his eyes soon me and Luke spent the whole day with Tulip cuddling and just down right having fun.

Luke's POV

It's been a year since we got Tulip, and thank God she's housebroken, life just got a little easier right now. Michael and I are watching. However, Michael had fallen asleep around two hours ago, and Tulip was in his lap, so he was very comfortable, but tonight was our movie marathon night. Michael sadly didn't make it through the second movie. Still, as I looked down at his sleepy face, I smiled and thought about what the future had in store for us. Michael mentioned that he wanted to have kids. I don't know how I feel about it. Honestly, Michael explained to me that there is a potion that will get him pregnant for nine months, but I don't know if I'm ready to be a dad yet, so I told him I'd think about it.

Then I felt Michael beginning to stir. He looked up at me and said, "did I pass out again? Sorry babe. I'm just really tired lately" I chuckle and say, "it's okay, angel face it's about time to hit the hay anyway, so come on" I then carried Michael upstairs bridal style. We got into our pj's Tulip then got into her little bed. We all went to bed. I woke up a little early, so I decided to get some work done in my office. Since we moved from new york, I had to get a new job. I'm now working as a stockbroker at Miko Corp, and right now, the business is profitable. Once I got all my work done, I went back to my bedroom and saw that Michael was gone. I then heard crying coming from the bathroom. I opened the door to see Michael on the floor, cutting himself. I quickly grabbed the knife and threw it across the floor and held Michael. The latter was crying hysterically. I then hushed his tears and began to carry him to our bed, where he settled down.

Michael then screamed "I'm so sorry Luke I never wanted you to see me like that please don't hate me" I then held Michael and said "what are you talking about I could never hate you angel face but what was that" Michael then sat up and said "Luke I cut myself in my sleep i don't know how i don't know why but i've been doing it since i was twelve and now you must think I'm a freak right and if you want me to leave i'll leave" I then held Michael close to my chest and kissed him furiously taking Michael's breath away making him completely forget all about being sad and when I ended the kiss i smiled at him and licked his cuts secreting my devil venom into the open wounds causing a slight crackling sound to resonate from them soon the cuts became clean and his skin returned to normal i then picked Michael up and placed him on my lap and began to nibble on his ear causing him to moan softly after I was done I then got close to Michael's ear and said "let's have a baby Angel face" Michael then began to blush as he felt my stiffy pop up between his legs Michael then took off his night shirt and stretched out his wings and he was prepared to be sore this morning.

The next morning I saw Michael was gone, and the same was for Tulip. I then heard Tulip barking outside, meaning she was in the backyard, which left Michael. I then followed the singing to the shower. Feeling a bit naughty, I snuck inside the bathroom, took off my clothes, and joined Michael, who didn't even notice me. I then kissed his shoulder, and he turned around and rested his head on my, and I placed my arms around his small twig-like body. We then kissed for what felt like hours, but it was just a few seconds. Still, the love shared between us was so strong that a second might as well be an hour. As the two of us got out of the shower, Michael then said, "I made us an appointment with the chemist lab weir meeting with her at six, so be ready" I nodded and went into our bedroom to put on some clothes I put on a t-shirt and sweatpants then went to go get Tulip.

As I let Tulip inside, I noticed that she was filthy, so I decided to give her a nice bath. I then took Tulip to our second bathroom and began to wash all the dirt and fleas off her. She was a good girl when it came to bathes she didn't fight at all. Still, when the bath was over, I wrapped her up in the fluffiest towel I had and quickly dried her. Off Tulip then went running out the bathroom like thunder, then I took a look at the clock and saw that it was almost three-thirty, so I went to my shared bedroom and saw Michael already getting ready. I quickly joined in. Soon we were both out the door.

As I started the car, I noticed Michael was looking at Gerber magazines. He was so ready for this, and who could blame him? He finally had a chance to live his own life, and I was proud of him for that, but the drive had already taken like two hours. So far, there was no traffic what so ever so it was clear skies. Still, soon we finally made it to the lab. As we got out of the car, we saw that the building was quite large, but soon Michael grabbed my hand and led the way into the lab where we saw the waiting room was almost vacant, but there was one girl with shimmering white hair and spectacles.

She looked up at us and smiled "well, hello, my name is Mel. I take it you have an appointment" we nodded. She leads us to the back room where she plucked a hair from my head and put it in a potion. She then took a blood sample from Michael and applied it to the brew. When it was complete, Mel gave the elixir to Michael and said, "now drink this and come back in two weeks for a checkup well till then."

As we drove home, I could tell Michael was a little uneasy about all that transpired in the building, but I placed my hand on his knee and gave him a comforting look that said, "don't worry. It'll be fine" for the rest of the night we relaxed and read books on the sofa.

Michael's POV

Well, we've been to Mel's lab twice, and she's sure of it I am pregnant. I even did some testing of my own to be confident, and it's for real. To think we'll be having a little bundle of joy soon, it's all so exciting. When Luke got Mel's okay, he immediately went to Babies "R" Us he bought all blue and white items. Of course and I even picked out the clothes, we even decided on a name for him. It's going to be Calum as for right now. I'm reading another Gerber magazine. At the same time, Luke set's up the nursery. I swear he's been working on it none stop. I'm glad sometimes when we cuddle at night. He rubs my extended belly. On occasion, Calum will kick it makes us both laugh when Calum pushes Luke's hand away with such vigor tee hee it's so cute. Suddenly, Luke walked inside, noticing me lying on the bed rather sloppily "now what would Calum think if he saw you like this" Luke said, crossing both of his arms. I then started to fix myself, and soon Luke smiled at me and sat next to me on the bed. He then kissed my cheek and neck, causing me to moan, then it was my turn. I then licked my lips and began to suck on his neck, making a beautiful violet mark. I then removed his shirt and rested my head on his soft, firm pecs, but I jumped up when I felt Calum kick, which caught me off,   guard.

Luke then placed his hand on my stomach and began to rub it slowly, causing Calum to settle and causing me to purr out of comfort, and then we heard barking coming from outside our door. It was just Tulip wanting to go into our room. Luke got up and let Tulip inside. She was a little bit bigger now and was now able to jump up on our bed. She seemed to understand what was going on with me because she would sniff and lick my belly every time I lay down. The cold, wet sensation would make me shiver slightly, but I would giggle every time, so it was very comforting. Luke even knew that my feet would hurt from time to time, so he would ease my pain by massaging them and soak them in bath salts. I would sometimes try to hide my problems, but Luke could see straight through me every time. I swear he's so loyal I love it.

I then start to doze off, and I hear Luke calling Tulip out of the room. So I can rest then before I drifted off completely, I feel Luke planting a kiss on my temple. Shortly after my nap, I see that Luke has brought dinner to me. I smiled at him. I quickly start eating as he flips through channels. We eventually find the Simpsons, and we settled on that. When I finished my meal, Luke took my tray and cleaned it up quickly. However, I still could sneak up behind him and say, "how much do you love me, Luke" Luke then turned around and held me and said, "angel face, I love you to the moon and back." "More," I whisper, "my love for you is a sword, and with it, I am all-powerful," Luke said, stroking my hair "more," I whisper again. "you are the loving sun, and I am the strong moon, soon our unified light will create a new light that being Twilight," Luke said, placing a hand on Calum. "One more time, my prince," I whisper again, allowing a tear to fall the ground, "my dear Michael is the only treasure that I shall never ruin you. I will instead love and protect you," Luke said, picking me up bridal style. I then placed my face into his pecs and softly cried. While whispering, "you make me feel so safe, Luke, you are my charming prince."
Luke then placed me on the bed and snuggled next to me. Luke then kissed me again, and I smiled as I started to fall asleep, feeling a small soft kick inside me. I guess Calum approves of our love. Which made me smile now I know the future's looking bright.

Two days later

I saw that Luke had already gone downstairs, so I decided to take a shower. As I was washing my hair, I started to sing a random song. As I sang, I started thinking about what Mel said. She said that my pregnancy was very fast-paced. I believe she said it would take three to six months for Calum to be born, but Luke knew about my worries, so he asked if Mel could make a house call, so that's today's goal.

As I got out of the shower, I heard Tulip barking witch meant Mel had arrived. I quickly got dressed, walked downstairs, and sat next to Luke, and I saw Mel sitting across from him. Mel then pulled out her devices and put the cream on my gut while preparing the ultrasound, and there he was, my baby. My sweet, sweet Calum alive and unharmed, I started crying tears of joy, and soon Luke wiped away my tears and kissed Calum. "I'd say it'll be any day now tee hee congrats," Mel said packing, up her stuff. Soon I got up and hugged Mel, and she hugged me back before she left.

Luke and I then took it easy for the rest of the day, but before I went to bed. Luke gave me a little present. It was a golden locket with Luke and me on one side and the other side reserved for Calum. I smiled at the cute gift and started to move closer to Luke. Soon I was sitting on his lap, giving him another one of my famous violet marks. Then, as I got up, I instantly came down to my knees, feeling intense pain. Then it dawned on me. I then turned to Luke and said, "babe, it's time we need to go," Luke nodded and carried me to the car. He then placed me in the back and drove like hell. When we got to the hospital, the nurses rushed to my side and took me to the er. Luke quickly put on some scrubs and came in and joined me.

Luke then grabbed my hand as I began to push soon, the pain was over, and I was holding Calum. He had my nose and his Father's eyes. Calum was so precious, but for a few moments, Calum wouldn't scream. I mean, his eyes were open, and Calum was blinking. He wouldn't cry finally. The nurse came and took Calum away from us but only when he left our arms. Calum immediately started to wail, and Luke quickly took Calum from the nurse, and Calum began to smile for the first time. Then Calum started to giggle the nurse then said. "I'm sorry, but we need to run a few checkups if that's okay" Luke knew it was the right thing to do, but he didn't want to see our baby boy cry like that again. So with a hesitant smile, he handed Calum to the nurse.

Calum immediately began to cry again. Luke then returned to me, his head low. I placed my finger on his cheek and said, "Hey, don't be like that. At least he is alive. That's what matters most" Luke immediately began to perk up for the next several hours. I laid there recuperating while Luke went to check up on Calum and what he told me. Calum was not having a great first day. His face kept getting redder and redder with each passing moment away from us. Once the nurse spotted Luke. I hear she handed Calum over to him right away. Once I saw the two of them, I smiled. Calum then started to coo and giggled in the embrace of his daddies. Luke and I both stared into each other's eyes and made a promise to protect our precious flower till the very end. It was midnight when we were able to leave the hospital with our new baby boy.

As we entered the house, we saw that Tulip was asleep on the sofa. We left her there and took our baby boy to his room. Luke turned on the lights while I got Calum dressed in a blue and white bunny onesie. Luke smiled as he looked over my shoulder and saw our cute baby boy. Calum was still in a half-sleep state, so I handed him over to Luke, who cradled him in his big strong arms. I then handed Luke a bottle and watched how he delicately slipped it into Calum's mouth. Calum looked so cozy in his Daddy's arms I just had to take a picture, so I pulled out my camera and snapped the pic then showed it to Luke. He gushed as he burped Calum than our thoughts weir interrupted by Calum's adorable burp, then we both gushed. It was so cute then we were reminded of our responsibility when Calum yawned. I then turned on the mobile while Luke rocked Calum to sleep and placed him in his crib. I then slipped one of the many dummies we had into Calum's lips, and we watched as he slept. It was so peaceful. That's when we slowly crept out of the room and cracked the door so that we could get to him anytime.

Calum's POV

I awoke in a completely new place that was unfamiliar to me. There was color everywhere, and I was wearing utterly unique attire. All I can remember was darkness, then a bright light. I was in two massive people's arms that made me feel safe and warm, but now I'm alone, and I want them to come back. I don't wanna be alone "WAAAAAAAAAAAAAAAA" I screamed, "I'm coming sweetheart," a voice yells out. Suddenly, I hear the door open and see a tall man with long golden hair walk in. He picks me up out of my prison and starts rubbing my back, "it's an okay, sweetheart. I got you," he says to me. He then starts bouncing me, and I start giggling a little, which causes him to laugh "let's have a check, then we can go downstairs and have num nums hmm," he says as he pats my bum causing me to giggle.

I giggled as the man brought to the large table. The man then placed me down onto the top of the table. He removed my blue and white clothes. Then there were two popping sounds, then the man lifted my legs into the air, and then I felt something cold for a second. Then I felt my bum land on something nice and fluffy. Then I heard the popping sound again. After that, the man sprinkled white powder over my legs and rubbed it in. It all felt so soothing. After the process, the man tickled me, placed a white shirt on me, and then put me on his shoulder and carried me through a long corridor and down some hills. That's when I saw another man who smiled at me and said. "Hey angel face, how's our little flower doing on his second day," he said as I hid my face in my holder's neck. Making my holder giggle, "he's fine. Would you care to feed him while I go take care of Tulip," he said as my holder handed me over to the man causing me to whine out of fear. The man then got me into a good position and put a weird thing in front of my face. The man tapped it against my lips a few times. I then opened my mouth. He placed the item inside. I then started to suck on it, and a smooth liquid came oozing out.

As the liquid went down my throat, I began to feel relaxed. Then as I looked up at my new holder, I noticed this one was different. This one had short purple hair and facial hair and pretty purple eyes. After a while, the liquid stopped flowing, and my belly felt funny. The man then placed me on his shoulder and began patting my back "come on, who's Daddy's, strong little man," he says to me as I reply with a burp, but I think this one's called Daddy then who's that other guy? Well, until I find out, I know this is Daddy. Soon that other man came back with another thing, this one was on all four legs and lots of hair, and it looked so strange.

The thing then started to sniff me and felt rather funny. I then grabbed at the thing's wet nose and giggled, and then the strange thing opened its mouth, and the peculiar thing's tongue licked me. I then look up and see Daddy and the other man laughing. I look at them and start to blush. Then Daddy hands me to the other holder and leaves, then I start to whine because I want Daddy, but he looks at me and says, "Don't worry, Calum Mommy's got you." I then looked up at the man holding me and tilted my head. He just stared at Daddy with a funny face. Then he looked down at me and smiled and said, "it's okay, Calum. He's just joking it's Papa, sweetheart" "no, it's not," Daddy yelled. Mommy just looked back at Daddy and said, "Luke come on" Daddy and Mommy just yelled at each other while I was placed on Mommy's hip, smiling all the while I didn't understand what they were fighting over. All I knew is that Mommy sounds better than Papa.

Luke's POV

As Michael and I argued, I noticed Calum was just happily giggling to himself. When Michael realized I wasn't paying attention, he saw what I was staring at, and he smiled. Then turned to me and said, "we can talk about this later right now, I think someone wants to play." Michael then handed Calum over to me and left to make lunch. I then looked down at my sweet baby boy and said. "what are we going to do with him, huh?" Calum then giggled, which caused me to chuckle. Then I carried Calum upstairs to my man cave. It was my office/workout room. The desk and computer were in the left corner of the room. While my barbels weir along the right wall next to the door. Then in the center of the room was my yoga mat, and in front of the office, the desk was a somewhat high window, and below that window was a little play area. For Calum, whenever I needed to do work and watch my son at the same time. However, today I decided to work out while playing with my boy today. So I got a soft quilt, put it at the yoga mat's head, and placed Calum on his back. Then I began to do some push-ups, but I nibbled at his soft tummy every time I got down to Calum's level, causing him to giggle and coo even more. It honestly made me lose track of how many I did, so I just shrugged and entertained Calum. I didn't even notice Michael stepping into the room, holding a camera in one hand and a bottle in the other I then heard a snap, which signaled me to stop. Then I picked up Calum and walked into our bedroom with Michael to change my sweaty clothes. As I reapplied deodorant in the bathroom mirror, I saw how cute Michael looked feeding our son. I swear it melted my heart. Then I heard a small yawn that sounded like a little kitten. I looked over and saw it was Calum Michael then smiled at me and said, "Hey babe, Calum's getting tired, so I'm going to put him down for a nap. See you soon" I nodded as Michael left the room.

When he came back, he hugged me and said, "best day ever, babe" I smiled as we both laid on the bed and cuddled. "angel face, what do you say we go to the park tomorrow, with Calum and Tulip" Michael squealed with excitement showing that he approved. Of my idea, then Tulip came into the room and jumped up on the bed and weaved her way between Michael and me. I just laughed and ruffled her fur with my hand causing her to lick my face. Michael just chuckled and rubbed her tummy.

After about a few hours of playing with our dog, we heard Calum whining in his room, thanks to the baby monitor. I then got up and walked into the nursery and saw that Calum had a wet diaper. I then cradled the boy and took him to the changing table to resolve his little problem. Once I changed Calum, I grabbed his dummy that rested in his crib and walked back to my room. Michael and Tulip were waiting. I laid down on my bed, placing Calum on my chest, and for a while, we just laid there relaxing, and occasionally playing

Tulip seems attached to Calum, and he is to her. It made Michael and I smile, knowing that they had such a close bond with each other, but soon it became five, and dinner was late by 3 minutes. So we scooted Tulip off the bed, and I carried Calum downstairs while Michael prepared dinner.

I turned on the TV and checked the weather channel. It was going to be clear skies for tomorrow, so after we all ate. I flicked through Netflix and found a simple movie To watch, but I felt Calum moving around slightly as I watched the movie. When I looked down, he was still as a rock, but he was at it again when I looked away. So I decided to fake sleep to see what he was doing when I laid back and stood still. He was back at it also, but he thought I was asleep, so now I saw what Calum was doing. Calum was exploring his body movements. It was so cute I then chuckled, which caused him to look up at me with a little pouty face. Calum's cute grumpy face made me chuckle more than Michael came in holding a bottle, and when Calum saw the bottle, His eyes lit up. Michael chuckled and handed me the bottle, and I fed it to Calum Michael then scooted close to me and rested his head on my shoulder. Then I saw that Calum started reaching for Michael's hair, and soon he snagged one. Then he started tugging at it, causing Michael to get annoyed. I think Calum noticed this and started pulling harder. "come on, sweetheart, not so hard Mommy can only take so much" soon, Michael began to unwind Calum's grip from his hair. I chuckled and placed my boy on my shoulder and pat his back until he burped.

Calum then giggled and cuddled into my chest. Michael then kissed his forehead, causing Calum to laugh. I then heard the timer go off eight minutes into the movie. I then placed Calum down on his play mat. He whined a little bit when he saw me walk away, but I came back and wiggled one of the mat's toys witch caught his attention, and Calum started going to town. I then walked into the kitchen, picked up my plate, and walked back into the living room with Michael, and we ate our dinner. We didn't even watch the movie I put on. We just stared at Calum and smiled at how much fun he was having. Then Tulip came into the room. She yawned and laid down on the rug next to Calum and just watched him. When Michael and I finished our meal, I picked up both plates and washed them in the sink. When I came back, I saw that Michael was holding Calum in his arms and humming a gentle tune.

I sat next to him and took a look at little Calum. He was happily sucking on his thumb. Then the phone rang, and I answered. It turns out my boss was going on a massive rant about where I was, and I had told him my husband had become biologically inseminated, but he didn't buy it. He gave me the time off, but I was doing most of my work from home, but he still wanted to see me, and if I didn't come to work in the morning. I'd lose my job, so I turned to Michael and said, "angel face. I have to be at work tomorrow, so we might have to reschedule that family walk for the time being" Michael just smiled and nodded. I smiled back and went upstairs to get ready for bed.

As I got in the shower, I thought about the day I had. It was so much fun. I mean, Calum is just a ball of sunshine, and I can't get enough of it. I love our family.

Calum's POV

When I opened my eyes, I saw that I was once again in my crib. I rubbed my eye with my hand and looked around. It was still dark out, but I needed changing, and I felt lonely, so I cried out for Mommy and Daddy. Then the door came open, and it was Mommy who smiled at me and said, "oh, what is it, baby boo" Mommy then placed me on the table and cleaned me up then he sat in the rocking chair then he started cradling me, humming that song I like. I'm soon asleep again, and when I wake up this time, its daylight, I'm lying in Mommy's arms. I giggle, which causes him to laugh than the weird thing comes in and sniffs me, and I giggle even more.

"Okay, baby boo, let's play for a little, then we can get you into a nice warm bath," Mommy said as he pulled out some object and started moving it around really fast in the air. It was entertaining to watch, then soon I wanted to try, so I reached out for it. Mommy giggled and gave me the thing and said, "does Calum want the stuffie? Hmm," I then let out a small whine answering Mommy's question. He giggled and handed me the stuffy, and I started feeling it. The stuffy was so soft and warm, and soon I shook it around, and it was so much fun. Soon I was being lifted into the air and taken to an all-white room with many weird things. Mommy then sat me on the cold ground and did something soon. A sound went on for a while, then Mommy turned to me and started removing my clothes. Then he picked me up in the air and placed me in a container with a clear liquid. That felt funny, then I saw this white fluffy stuff and scooped it up, and when I brought my hands down into the liquid, there was a fun splash. So I did it, again and again., I didn't even notice Mommy washing me with some strange things. I was having too much fun then I heard another noise that seemed to be scaring away the liquid. I tried to chase after it, but it kept running away, and then a slow chill started to run up my back.

Mommy then got a long, fluffy thing and wrapped it around my tiny body and lifted me into the air. Mommy started rubbing the soft thing all over me, and it felt so lovely. After a few seconds, Mommy wrapped me up in the fluffy thing and carried me to my room. Mommy then laid me on the table and undid the soft thing and got me dressed. Mommy then smiled down at me and kissed my head, and I giggled. Mommy then held me in his arms and brought me down the stairs to the living room. Mommy placed me on my play mat and said, "okay little one enjoy some tummy time while Mommy does the dishes," he cooed as he turned on the tv and left the room.

I wasn't watching the TV so much that I was paying attention to the colors, but soon I heard something open followed by "Michael, I'm home. Where's my little man" then I knew who it was it's Daddy once I see him I started giggling and squealing. Daddy smiles at me and picks me up, and I grab hold of his shirt. "Why, hello Calum, how are we today," Daddy asked. I squeal to try and show that I'm fine, then Mommy comes into the room "hi babe, how was work" Mommy asked, "fine, everything went surprisingly, smooth" Daddy replied they didn't even notice that I was messing around with Daddy's pretty necklace.

Soon Mommy and Daddy kissed, and Daddy put me on his shoulder and sat on the couch. Then Daddy moved me to his lap, then Daddy looked down at me and smiled and started tickling my tummy for a few moments. Then I had an accident and whined. Daddy then looked down at me, concerned, but he caught on soon enough, then he placed me on his shoulder and took me upstairs to the table in my room. Once I was fresh, we came back downstairs and sat on the couch. Then the weird thing went into the living room and laid down on the floor.

Then Mommy came into the room and said, "Hey babe, why don't we go for a walk? I think it's a nice day outside" Daddy nodded in approval and took me upstairs and got me dressed in a baby blue shirt that read Daddy's boy. Then he topped it off with white shorts and pale blue booties. Once Daddy finished dressing me, Daddy took me to his room and laid me on his bed and left soon, I got lonely. I started to whine, then Mommy came in and held me close. He seemed to have a white wool sweater instead of his t-shirt. I cuddled into Mommy's chest. It felt so warm then Daddy came in and said, "okay, we are all set" Mommy nodded and said, "yep, Tulip's already set up and waiting downstairs."

Soon Daddy took Tulip's thingy, and Mommy held me on his hip. Then we were out the door where I got to see the world. There were other people outside playing, and some of them were looking at me. I got scared and hid my face in Mommy's chest. Mommy then looked down at me and said, "Oh sweetheart, it's okay Mommy and Daddy are here you'll be okay." Mommy then planted a kiss onto my head, causing me to giggle and reveal my face. We walked for a while. Then we sat at a bench; the walk had made me tired, so I yawned. Mommy then patted my back and started to hum. I then heard Daddy hum along. I felt so relaxed with the soothing cool breeze blowing through my hair and Mommy's chest's warmth, holding me close and safe, and then I fell asleep. When I woke up, I was in my crib. I stared at the mobile above me for a while. Then the door came open to reveal Daddy and Mommy; they looked down at me and said, "hi, little prince" Mommy then picked me up, and

Daddy came close and kissed me. I felt so loved then Mommy put me back in the crib. I started to whine, but then Mommy and Daddy pulled out many toys and played with me. It was so much fun.

After a while, I got tired again, and I think Mommy and Daddy noticed this, so Daddy placed a dummy in my mouth and then started the mobile. Soon the gentle tune began to play. The last thing I noticed was Mommy stroking my cheek with his finger then; I was out.

Time Skip

Luke's POV

As Michael and I left the room, we heard cute little snoring, which made us smile. We then walked downstairs and sat on the couch. Michael pulled out his sketchpad and started drawing while I let Tulip outside for a little bit. She was a sweet dog and very loving. On top of that, I then went to the fridge to get a drink. Once I got my drink, I sat next to Michael and took a look at what he saw drawing. It was a cute picture of Calum that made my heart melt. I kissed Michael, causing him to blush "you know you're the sweetest Devil alive ya know that," Michael said, looking over at me, I returned the gaze and said, "and you are the Cutest Angel alive. I mean, look at you're so perfect kind, and handsome you're flawless" Michael began to blush, even more, turning bright pink. Soon tears formed in his eyes. I then hugged him, "Hey, it's okay, Angel Face you, and I both know you're perfect, and nothing will change. That okay," I whispered into his ear. Michael then began to calm down. He then kissed me.

"You always know what to say to me, babe, you're so kind," Michael said, looking into his Luke's eyes. When we heard Tulip pawing at the back door, I sat up and kindly let her inside. When I came back, I saw that Michael was gone when I called for him, it was silent. I then heard giggles coming from upstairs and went to investigate. I soon found myself in front of my shared bedroom, and when I opened it, I saw Michael holding a pleased Calum "oh look, Calum, it's Daddy," Michael said as Calum turned around and squealed at me, making grabby hands.

I then crawled beside Michael and lifted Calum into my arms, causing him to squeal. I then laid him on my chest and watched as he wiggled around. Michael giggled as Calum explored more of his movements then a foul stench reached my nose. I then got up and held Calum arm's length away from me. Michael then got up and placed a diaper mat on the edge of the bed. I laid Calum down on it, pulled the needed supplies out of the side drawer, and changed Calum. Once my little prince was all fresh and clean, I placed Calum on my shoulder and bounced him while Michael took another snapshot of Calum and me. I sighed when my vision returned. It seemed like since we first brought Calum home Michael's turned into his paparazzi. He even made a scrapbook and another, for every month he's been with us. I then walked over to Michael and kissed him on the cheek.

Calum must have noticed this because he quickly squealed. This imparticular squeal was his "hey, pay attention to me" squeal me, and Michael chuckled and went downstairs, where we sat on the couch together. Michael then pulled out a plush bear for Calum and gave it to him. Calum quickly grabbed it and started cuddling with it. I didn't feel like cooking tonight, and neither did Michael, so we decided to go out. We then went back upstairs to get dressed. Michael prepared a diaper bag all set up, and I got Calum dressed in the cutest little outfit. It was a white shirt with my little Angel's words in big purple bubble letters, and I put him in overalls and cute little brown booties. After that, we put Tulip's dinner in her dish. Then I put Calum in his playpen while I got dressed and came downstairs. I saw Michael was waiting for me in a white dress shirt and white jeans. I had the same attire, but mine was all black. Soon I grabbed my keys, and Michael picked up Calum and his diaper bag, and we left out the door and walked to the car. Michael buckled in Calum while I started the car, and we drove to the nearest restaurant. It was a family place known as the Breezy Cloud.

We quickly got Calum and got out of the car and walked inside. As soon as we got in, we saw lots of kids and super bright lights. Calum took in everything. The lights the sounds, and he was squealing. Soon a waitress led us to our booth. We didn't want to get a booster seat because we wanted to feel closer to Calum. So he sat in Michael's lap. I then quickly grabbed a dummy out of Calum's bag. Michael put it in his cute little mouth. Calum suckled on it, occasionally bobbing it in and out of his mouth. While Calum was distracted, I took Michael's hand and said, "you know my parents have been calling to check in on us." Michael looked surprised, "well, what have they been asking," I saw Michael trembling. I held his hand and said, "babe, don't worry. They want to come and visit us," Michael began to calm down. Then I saw a little puddle slide across the table when I looked down and saw Calum with his head on the table and suckling on Michaels's hand. Michael soon looked and chuckled, "sweetie, you bored of your dummy already" when Michael removed his hand Calum started to whine and soon woke up. Michael then placed the dummy back into his mouth. Still, Calum spat it out and started crying. Michael then placed Calum on his shoulder and started patting his back; I went into the bag and handed Michael a bottle. Michael tried to feed him, but Calum just fussed even more.

Michael then patted Calum's diaper, and he wasn't wet or messy. He was just fussy. I could see Michael growing more and more agitated, so I took Calum from him and told him to go outside and chill. He nodded. I then placed my lips against Calum's forehead. He was burning up. I then called the waitress and told her to get to-go boxes for us. After that, I waited and took the bags and left. I ran into Michael, and he saw my concerned face "what's wrong babe," he said. I frowned and kissed Calum's head. "Calum seems to be sick. I got the food so let's go home."

Calum's POV

I haven't been sleeping. I don't want to sleep, and I want this pain to go away. It hurts so much I want Mommy to make me feel better. I want my Mommy. I start screaming at the top of my lungs, and Mommy and Daddy run in. Mommy picks me up and holds me "hows he feels, babe" I hear Daddy say Mommy kisses my head. I start to calm down a little "Calum's not as hot as he was before. I think he's getting better, but can you get some medicine and draw a cold bath for him," Mommy said, cradling me as Daddy left the room. Mommy then removed my Pajamas, and Mommy held me in his arms. I started to feel a little better until I got sweltering again.

I then screamed again. Mommy rubbed my back and said. "I know, baby boo, I know you feel icky, but we're doing all we can to help you shh shh you're going to be okay, sweetie." I stopped screaming and started whimpering, showing I was a little calmer. "there want a drink, baby boo," Mommy said, holding a water bottle. I opened my mouth, allowing Mommy to place the bottle inside. Mommy then took me to the white room and gave me to Daddy, who gave Mommy a strange jar filled with something. Then Mommy left Daddy, then removed my diaper and placed me in the water. It felt so soothing, and then Daddy started washing me. When the bath was over and done with, Daddy wrapped me up in a towel, carried me to my room, and started putting a diaper on me. Then he wrapped me up in a fluffy blankie and took me downstairs, and we sat on the couch and cuddled. I still felt icky. I stared up at Daddy with pain in my eyes, just wanting him to take the problem away. Daddy rubbed my cheek with his finger and said, "I know you feel bad, Calum, but Mommy and I are doing all we can to make you feel better. Just hang on, okay" I started to suck on my thumb and relax a little.

Then Mommy came in and whispered something into Daddy's ear. I wanted to know, so I started to whine. I calmed down when Mommy gave Daddy a bottle. It had this blue liquid, and I started reaching for it. Mommy and Daddy chuckled before Daddy. Gave me the bottle, and It tasted weird. It wasn't bad either it helped a lot, but I soon grew sleepy again, and I slowly went out like a light.

Michael's POV

We sat there, watching our little boy sleep. He was so cute. Luke then kissed my face. "Thanks for helping him, babe, look how content he is," Luke said, causing me to blush. "It was for our baby boo, and all I did was add one of my feathers to water, turning it into holy water and since Calum is a half breed. I knew it would have a positive effect," I explained. Luke gave me a gentle kiss and said. "still, you're the sweetest Mommy alive." for the rest of the night, we cuddled with our son. Until the clock hit ten, we all fell asleep on the couch when I saw the morning. That Luke was gone, and I could hear Calum snoring on the baby monitor. That meant the holy water was working. Luke had to be at work. I stretched and made some coffee.

I then noticed that Tulip was going upstairs, probably to check on Calum. I smiled and decided to do some housework. After a while, I heard Calum wake up. I checked on him, and I saw Tulip sitting next to the crib staring at Calum, and he was staring at her Tulip then licked his cute little hands, causing Calum to giggle. It warmed my heart seeing my baby happy I then picked him up and patted his bum. He had a wet one. It was so cute. I then put him on the table and changed him. After that, I undressed him and put a green romper on him nice and snug. I then picked Calum up and carried him downstairs, where I placed him on the playmat while I started cleaning again, but soon the doorbell rang. I checked the peephole and saw it was my Father. I instantly started to hyperventilate, but I regained my composure and took Calum into the nursery to be safe from my Father's gaze. I could hear Tulip barking at the door, something she never did. I got worried

I opened the door a crack and said. "what do you want" I said, shooting daggers at the man, "I want to see my son. How have you been," Father said. I quickly closed the door and turned. On the stereo, my Father kept banging on the door more, and more and soon, Calum started crying. I went upstairs to soothe him thankfully. My Father left, but I would be telling Luke later, but then the doorbell rang again. Tulip then started barking again. Witch scared me. I then grabbed a diaper bag and my phone and was prepared to make a getaway out. Then there was a banging at the door. I then knew it was my Father, so I quickly grabbed a leash for Tulip and ran out the back door holding a panicking Infant in my arms. We ran for about two blocks and reached the forest. I was out of breath, and Calum was so terrified I felt his tush and Calum was utterly soaked. I rubbed his back and sang a lovely song that soothed him. Once Calum was calm, I instantly looked around and saw that I was in the middle of the forest. I sighed and pulled out a changing mat for Calum and quickly changed him. I then dug a small hole, placed the diaper inside it, burying it, and gave the soil nutrients. I then picked up Calum and the changing mat and started walking with Tulip to exit this forest, hopefully.

I soon found my way back in town, but I knew I was close to Luke's office. I recognized the area and made my way to the building dog in tow, but Tulip was a smart dog. She would usually give us a hint of when she needed to go. We found Luke in the office, and boy was he surprised I kissed him, and he took Calum from me and cuddled with him, causing Calum to squeal happily. "umm babe, we need to talk," I said. Luke nodded and said, "sure about what" I then told him about my Father's surprise visit, and Luke became furious. He kept his cool for Calum's sake. I started crying. Luke came by my side with Calum even Tulip joined in. Calum started whimpering. He didn't like seeing us upset he was such a sweet child. Luke then kissed my head. I kissed him back. Tulip even started licking my hand. All this support made me smile, and it was all so lovely we stayed in Luke's office for the rest of the day. Until he finished work, then we all got in his car and drove home. We grabbed a bite before going home.

When we got in the Driveway, I started shaking Luke then kissed me and took out his pistol and entered the house. I held my phone for dear life, ready to call the police.

Luke's POV

As I entered the house, I felt an angry aura resonate off the walls, and I was surprised. Everything was still intact. Thankfully I did a sweep of the house and saw that all was well. I then called Michael. Soon they came inside, I put my gun away and went downstairs to greet my Family Michael. I sat on the couch with Calum in his lap "babe, I think we need to move away from here," I suggested. Michael nodded, so we agreed not to discuss it. Further, at least until Calum took his nap, we would discuss this at great length then.

Two days passed, and we had already found a place in Paris. It was a wonderful house in the countryside. My brother, who lives in France, got me a job at his shop matter of fact, my whole family lives in Paris, and they were so excited to see Michael and Calum. I was a tad bit nervous. My family was a little odd. They had no idea that Michael was an Angel, so I didn't know how they would react to him, not that they had anything wrong against Angels. They just never got close to them in a familial way. I guess anyway we would be boarding the plane in a few hours, so we had just finished packing our belongings and are now getting Tulip in her crate, and thankfully Calum is still asleep; hopefully, he'll stay that way. We then called a cab and loaded everything onto it. We then drove to the airport, and we then boarded our plane, and to our surprise. Calum was still asleep; that is until we took to the air, then Calum began to shiver and shake.

Michael then cradled him, and I hummed a gentle tune. All this made Calum coo with contentment, and he was calm for the rest of the ride. Calum wasn't fussing at all. He was a perfect little lamb, and that deserved a reward. I picked up my little man and pulled out his paci, but I slathered it in some of my devil venoms before giving it to him. Since Calum had my DNA, my toxin wouldn't harm him; instead, it would be like breast milk. To him, but when we were in Atlantia, I slipped some of my venoms into his bottles.

Michael didn't know, but I had been preparing for this day. I then suckered Calum's paci in devil venom, so I placed the paci in Calum's mouth with a happy smile. When Calum suckled on it, he began to coo and giggle a lot. Michael looked over at our very excited son and raised a brow "Luke, what did you do to our son," Michael asked. I chuckled and shrugged and patted Calum's head "are you sure he's super hyper? I'm not too fond of it. What did you do" Michael said, staring at me with a worried glare sadly. I couldn't lie to him when he stares like that, "babe. It's okay. I just soaked his paci in my venom, and I've also been sneaking venom into his bottles at night. No big deal," I said. Michael then started to glare at me. "Luke, you know as well as I do that your venom is like sugar water to him. It's not healthy for him; you could get him sick." Michael said, picking up our delighted baby boy who was still giggling.

"angel face look, he's so happy he loves his Daddy's venom. Can you honestly say no to that cute face, huh can you," I said, pointing to our cute boy. Michael looked down and gave a loving coo. "Fine, but not every day, only when he's super good, we don't want you to start getting spoiled right, baby boo," Michael said, tickling Calum, who squealed more a few hours later. Calum crashed from his sugar high and was now soundly napping. Michael then began to stroke his back soothing him peacefully. Michael looked up at me and said, "did you do that on purpose because you knew he would fall asleep" I chuckled and kissed Michael zipping my lips, causing Michael to sigh.

When we landed, we got our things and met with my Father Damien Moto. he saw Michael and looked him over. He smiled and said, "okay, let me help you guys with your bags" Dad and I then loaded the car. Simultaneously, Michael took Calum inside the car and cuddled him once Dad and I finished. We got in the car as well. Dad looked at Calum in the back seat and said. "He's cute. How old is the little guy?" Michael blushed "his name is Calum. He's 23 hehe he's our special baby boo," Michael said, kissing Calum's head. Calum then began to stir and wake up. He rubbed his eyes and looked around "hi, little one. Mommy's glad to see that you are awake," Michael said. Dad looked back and said, "Mommy?" I then explained to my Dad that we decided that Michael would be the Mommy. Since he was the more feminine out of the two of us, Calum spotted my Dad stared at him intently. Michael bumped his nose and said, "that's pop, pop. Calum, say hi, sweetie" Calum whined and hid his face into Michael's chest. Dad just laughed, and soon we made it to my family home. It was a large house with a working windmill in the back.
"You grew up here?" Michael asked. I then let Tulip out of her crate and said, "yes, the windmill is a remnant of the human village. That once stood here, they left because they feared the war, but when the Humans tried to return, they soon found the place inhabited by Devils. This village was the foothold needed to make France the Kingdom of Devils hehe ever since we Devils have completely cleaned up France's history, making it the greatest country. My family, the Moto's, helped reconstruct the first city of Devils Moto Drasil. Named after my Great Grandfather Drake Moto," I explained. We then walked inside the house, where I saw my brother Claude. He was similar to me, but he was shorter than me and was very skinny. You could mistake him for an Angel. He was so proper and kind when most Devils are intimidating and manly, but my brother is meek and sort of a sissy, so he didn't have a perfect childhood. I

would usually have to fight for him a lot sigh, but Claud would spend most of his time mending my wounds with Devil venom. I swear Devil venom does wonders for injuries.

Dad then sat on the couch next to Claude, startling him, but when he saw us, he jumped up and ran to me, giving me the biggest hug he could give. Then he saw Michael and shook his hand, and when he saw Calum, he gushed. "nice to see you, big bro, and your son is adorable," Claud said, taking us to the sitting room Tulip followed us and laid in front of the fireplace. Calum was still a little uneasy around all these new faces, but he was starting to get comfortable, then I could hear it the gentle footsteps of my mother. She was a gentle Devil. With a lot of love and beauty to match, she saw me and ran to me, holding me tightly. My face became forcefully buried in her absurdly large breast. "hi Lukey oooh, I missed you so much," my Mom said, practically choking me with her monstrous grip, but if you were 523 years old, you would be absurdly strong too. She then loosened her grip and spotted my husband and child. Mom then kneeled in front of Calum, who just stared at her. He was slightly shaking, afraid of what my Mom would do but instead of being over the top like she usually is. Mom booped Calum's nose and said, "Hi, little one. I'm Nanna; it's so good to see you" Calum then reached out for Mom finally. She replied by picking him up and cuddling him close. Calum then received fifty kisses from my Mom. It was insane the amount of love she was giving him. I remember she did this to Claud a lot when he was little hehe maybe this is why he's so timid around women. Anyway, after a few moments, Calum began to whine, showing that he was 100% done with being coddled soon, he started whimpering, and Michael quickly took him from my Mom. Who pouted when she lost hold of her new grandson, but she calmed down and sat next to us, mainly watching Calum. As he was getting bottle-fed, smiling all the while, Claude was reading, and Michael was happily enjoying this time with our son. I enjoyed the time spent with everyone hehe for the rest of the day. We talked until dinner mom had made a spread for us, and it was marvelous. It then came time to turn in it seemed like a hassle to get everything out of the car and bring it into a house that wasn't going to be ready for some time, so we went upstairs to my old bedroom to take a load off Dad even set up my old cradle for Calum who was already asleep. I took him from Michael, changed him out of his day clothes, and put him into a fresh diaper. I then laid him in the cradle and watched as Calum squirmed in his sleep, investigating his new surroundings. I then placed my finger into his hand, and he settled down comforted by his Daddy's loving touch. Calum even started to smile a little.

Michael then came over and smiled at what he saw. Soon Michael put his finger in Calum's other hand, and soon it was clenched when Michael and I removed our fingers, Calum started to cry, and it broke our hearts. This cry was Calum's "please don't leave me" scream. I picked him up, and he settled down. I kissed my little prince and placed him on the bed next to Michael, who put him in between our pillows and kissed his little tummy. I came back shirtless in my pajama bottoms and got under the covers with my husband, who was still messing with our little prince. I joined in, and we managed to tire our little prince out. Soon he was snoring and sucking on his paci. Michael and I then stared at one another, and we cuddled, careful not to crush our little prince. We then fell asleep when I woke, up I saw that my husband and son still asleep I smiled and got up carefully not to disturb them, but when I reached for the door, I saw Calum whining for me getting ready to cry again. I came back and picked him up and cuddled him. He woke up dry, so he had to be in a good mood. I took him downstairs and saw that my mother had bottles already made up.

I then took one, shook it up, and gave it to Calum, who suckled on it happily. It made me smile at how content he was. Hehe soon, my Mom walked in smiling "hehe, how is my little bunny" she said, looking over my shoulder "he's fine Mom, he's just happy," I said, bouncing my baby boy, who smiled even more "can I take Calum once he's finished eating" my mother asked practically jumping in place. I nodded, and when Calum was full. I burped him and handed him to my Mom, who proceeded to take him to the living room where they played together. I could tell she enjoyed being with her grandson. I loved watching them, and I could tell Calum loved it too. I chuckled and started making coffee for Michael and me. I carried both mugs upstairs and sat on the bed as Michael got up "morning angel face, how did you sleep" I said, handing him the coffee "good where's Calum" Michael asked, looking worried "he's with my Mom downstairs" Michael smiled it was rare to have some time alone without Calum. We loved him, but we wanted to be alone sometimes.

We then started to cuddle, then Tulip came in and rested at our feet. Tulip snuggled in place, and Michael laughed at the warmth she gave off. I swear Michael was like a giant child at times. It made me feel so happy soon we got dressed and ready for the day. When we came downstairs, we saw that Mom was holding Calum, who was happily napping hehe. "Mom, I'm going to start breakfast if that's okay?" I said. Mom responded by nodding as I was cooking, I could see Tulip running around outside. She was blissfully content. Michael then came into the room and smiled at me. "so what are you cooking," Michael asked. I shrugged and said, "well, it's just pancakes and sausage, and, to top it off, scrambled eggs hehe" Michael then came over and kissed my face. I kissed back, and then we heard Calum start to cry. Mom came in, holding our upset little prince. It seemed she couldn't settle him down. Michael then took Calum from my Mom. Calum was still agitated but was beginning to settle down. Michael then rubbed his back and whispered his favorite song. Calum then began to coo, which meant he was utterly calm. Michael then took Calum to the living room, and Mom stayed and said that Dad was busy preparing our house and that it was almost complete in about an hour. He worked late into the night to finish up our home, and frankly, I was glad soon we would be in our own house in France. Hehe, I can't believe I'm home. It's been so long, and I'll be starting my own business. It's going to be a little flower shop since I was a flower enthusiast. I went to school for Botany for some time, so I had a few tricks up my sleeves when it came to flowers. I could even start a garden in the backyard. That would be how we got our primary source of income hehe. Anyway, I finished breakfast, I called everyone in, and I set the plates. I then passed out the food and gave some to everyone. Well, Calum got pancakes, and my Mom mostly fed him when everyone Finished breakfast, and my Mom had cleaned Calum's face of syrup. We went into the living room and watched tv Calum didn't understand what was going on, so he mostly babbled to himself with the occasional coo now and then. Soon Dad came in with a proud smile and said, "okay, the house is complete. I even moved all the furniture into the new house. Hehe," Michael and I smiled and got up to go pack our stuff. I could tell my mother was pouting because she couldn't smother her grandson anymore, but I knew she could come over and visit anytime hehe as soon as everything got packed up, we got in Dad's car drove to the new house. Calum was happily looking out the window and seeing all there is to see.

Third person's POV

As the years rolled by, Michael Luke and Calum became the closest family. Calum soon went to school, and he was doing reasonably well. Calum even started to grow angel wings, so Calum did take after his Michael. He's still calling Michael Mom, lol, but our story picks up on Calum's 90th birthday. Luke and Michael promised him something special hehe but they didn't tell him what it was, so they planned to surprise him.

Michael's POV

Luke and I are planning on having another baby soon, mainly because we don't like the idea of having an empty household. I know Calum is only 90, but the idea still looms over me, so I already went to the clinic, and now it's a waiting game. Luke is setting up the nursery, while Calum is at a friend's house. Hehe, we're taking him out to dinner, tonight where we'll tell him the news and give him his gifts. So in the meantime, I'm looking at Gerber Magazines while thinking of names for our future joy bundle. I'm wondering what it will be since Calum is an angel. Would this next child be a Devil? Hmm, oh, the possibilities we haven't painted the new nursery yet, but hey, we like surprises. Still, we will be getting an ultrasound in a few months once the baby's developed more sigh. I hope Calum takes the news well, but I hope my family doesn't come near us. I just want to live in peace with my family. That is all I want. The phone soon starts to ring, and I get up to answer it. I soon find out it's my sister. I start telling her all about the things she missed, like the birth of Calum. When she heard we had a child, Mimiru gushed with excitement. I then asked her if she'd like to visit. She humbly said no, saying she was taking care of Mother and Father, but I could care less those people never once cared about me, so to hell with them for all I care. For the rest of the conversation, we mainly planned a visit to her home in America.

That's when Calum walked in. He was covered entirely with mud, typical for him. I ended the phone call with my sister and ran over and hugged Calum. "Calum, why are you all dirty," I asked Calum. Chuckled and said, "my friends wanted to have a mud fight, and I won" at the mere mention of the word fight, I immediately started investigating Calum's body. There were a few scrapes here and there but nothing too major looking for signs of bruises or pain. I could feel Calum squirming around giggling. I'm glad he found this funny, but anyway, I told Calum to go upstairs and get ready for his bath. That I had to prepare and, of course, the word bath's mere mention caused Calum to run upstairs to his room and lock it. I sighed, but at least he'd be distracted for the time being. I went to start the bath, and soon I filled the tub was with water. I then stretched out my wings, plucked one of my feathers, and added it to the tub. So it would mend his wounds.

After that, I went to get Calum and low and behold. Calum still had the door locked. I plucked another one of my feathers and used it as a lock pick. When I got inside, I saw my little prince he was playing his video games. As soon as he saw me, he jumped, but then I gave him a look that said, "stop the foolishness now, young man," and the result was always the same complete obedience. Calum then sighed and went to the bathroom where he took his bath; meanwhile, I checked on the new nursery. It was going very well. We mainly handed down Calum's old toys and baby items, but we did have to buy some new ones. Still, the nursery was perfect.

Luke then kissed my side. I smiled and kissed back. After that, we got ready to go out to dinner. Luke loaded the gifts into the car, so we mainly waited in the living room until Calum was thoroughly prepared to come down in his dress shirt and jeans. "Okay, Calum, are you ready to go out," Luke said to Calum, who smiled widely and nodded. I then got up, and soon we made our way to the car, and I could practically feel Calum's excited heart jump up and down from inside him. Calum's excitement made me smile. We drove to a family restaurant and parked the car. When we got out, we walked into the restaurant, and a waitress escorted us to our table. We ordered our food and waited for our dinner. It was then when Luke left to get the presents. I smiled at Calum. I said, "Calum, when your father gets back, we have some big news to tell you" Calum smiled and said, "hehe okay mom, I can't wait" soon, Luke came back with a whole ten gifts and after opening them revealing that they were, in fact, several video games a bunch of books and other things.

Soon our food came, followed by a nice lovely strawberry cake. Once we ate the cake, we talked to Calum about how we wanted another baby. He seemed a little upset initially, but soon he smiled and yelled, "yay, I'm going to be a big brother!!!!!" me and Luke chuckled and continued to have a good time. When we got home, we had even more fun, and by the time Calum was asleep, Luke and I decided to have some fun of our own I smiled as Luke released his horns and tail and claws then beckoned me forth I slowly came over to him thinking of, what he would do to me my hard on getting more significant. Luke then took off his shirt, and I saw his muscles pulse, our powerful instincts resonating with each other. I suddenly fell into his arms, and my legs buckled. I couldn't stand it. I needed Luke inside me; Luke pushed me on the bed. With one quick snatch, he yanked off my clothes. Luke then got on top of me, my cock sticking straight up, and with one hand, Luke started to massage my balls, and I moaned loud enough to wake the dead. I curled my toes and clenched my fists. This euphoria was what I needed. I needed more "no no no, Luke, you can't cum yet hehe" Luke smiled. Still, I nodded, knowing it would be too soon. Luke started to lean over me, his warm, healthy body filling me with so much euphoria. Then he began to kiss me like a Mad man.

I responded by kissing back. I loved every minute of this. Luke then got up and got some toys. He tied a gag around my mouth. Then Luke started to push his Snake inside me with the speed and power of a drill. My ass felt like it would fall apart, but soon Luke started to get aggressive, and it was so excellent. Luke told me to hold my cum, but it was slowly beginning to leak out. It was so hard to keep it in soon my moaning filled the whole house. Thankfully, Calum was a deep sleeper, "OH GOD, I'M SOOOOO CLOSE," Luke yelled, and I moaned more. I soon grew numb and started to cum quickly, an ocean fell out of me, and I smiled, but I knew I would be in trouble, but who the fuck cares when I finished, Luke saw the cum and smiled. Knowing I had to be severely punished by this incredibly attractive Devil. Luke left to get something giving me a chance to rest when he came back. He was holding duck tape and a massive vibrator. I started to whine and cringe, but I was more concerned with the little life growing inside me. Luke saw the fear in my eyes and said, "it's okay. It won't hurt the baby, I promise," I trusted Luke, so I let Luke play with me with a gentle sigh. Soon, he tapes my wrists to my ankles and inserts the vibrator inside me. He set the setting to pervert, and I felt the urge to cum again. I loved it, and soon I passed out from all the pleasure.

Soon morning came, and I found myself freed from my binding, and I immediately went to the shower. I got cleaned up when I went to get dressed and when I went downstairs. I saw Luke and Calum watching tv. I smiled and joined them. We saw a news report about this cult of humans rebelling against the Angels and Devils. It seemed the police were handling it well, but it still worried me soon. A few hours passed, and we had had a little family time, that is, until we went out for breakfast, we went to Sir Charles Burger Castle. After that, we went to the park, but as we walked down the trail, I started feeling a pain soon, and I couldn't stand. "Michael, what's wrong," Luke yelled. Calum grabbed my side. I couldn't say anything soon I was being carried, and we ran to the car. When we got buckled in, we rushed to the hospital, and soon a nurse leads me to the ER.

Luke's POV

I could only watch as the nurses took my husband. I held Calum's hand tight, thinking of what could have caused this wait. Could it have been last night? Oh my god, I heard crying and soon realized it was Calum. I bent down and hugged him tightly. "Dad, is Mom going to be okay," he said. I smiled and said yes but of course. I was a bit unsure, but I knew I had to be Strong. Calum and I are currently in the waiting room where we sat waiting, but we had a lot of faith, so we knew things couldn't go wrong. Soon we saw the news, and apparently, the new cult had been causing an uproar, and it was getting out of control, then I saw this hospital show up on the screen. Anger and my family's wellbeing filled my mind, and I picked up Calum and ran to the ER, where I began looking for my husband soon. I heard a crash, and I also heard bullets and the sound of screams. It was the sound of the Humans fighting with my kind. I didn't care Michael and Calum were my main concern when I found him. I saw a nurse taking Michael taken up to another floor. Soon my feelings surged, and I couldn't handle it anymore. I ran to Michael's room and dropped off Calum, and I went to combat these vile humans who would dare harm my family. I soon gave in to my urges and fully transformed and attacked every single one.

To be continued

Made in the USA
Middletown, DE
22 April 2021